Designed by Flowerpot Press in Franklin, TN.
www.FlowerpotPress.com
Designer: Stephanie Meyers
Editor: Katrine Crow
ROR-0808-0110
ISBN: 978-1-4867-1264-9
Made in China/Fabriqué en Chine

THERE
was a
CROOKED
MAN

MELISSA EVERETT

Illustrated by
MARK KUMMER

He bought
a CROOKed cat
and they met
a CROOKed mouse.

And now
they all live
TOGETHER
in a
CROOKED
little
house.

The CROOKED cat is a MAGICIAN and can cut the mouse in HALF.

Together they do
CROOKed SHOWS,
and the
PEOPLE pay
them MONEY.

A CROOKED mouse
and CROOKED man

prove that DIFFERENT can be AWESOME. I hope you AGREE with that!